KISS A ME

To the Rescue

Babette Douglas

Illustrated by
Barry Rockwell

Productions

Kiss A Me™ Productions, Inc. produces toys and booklets for children with an emphasis on love and learning. For more information on how to purchase a Kiss A Me collectible and plush toy or to receive information on additional Kiss A Me products, write or call:

Kiss a me™ Productions

Kiss A Me Productions, Inc.
90 Garfield Ave.
Sayville, NY 11782
888 - KISSAME
888-547-7263

About the Kiss A Me Teacher Creature Series:
This delighfully illustrated series of inspirational books by
Babette Douglas has won praise from parents and educators alike.
Through her wonderful "teacher creatures" she imparts profound lessons of tolerance
and responsible living with heartwarming insights and a humorous touch.

KISS A ME To the Rescue

Written by Babette Douglas
Illustrated by Barry Rockwell

ISBN 1-89034-311-0
Printed in China

www.kissame.com

To a great rescuer...
Theresa M. Santmann

Preface

*In our wonderful and ever-changing world,
children are our greatest legacy
and investment in the future.
And yet, in the world we have prepared for
them, love seems to have been mislaid.*

*With this little story, one of a series, one
little creature, Kiss A Me, seems to have
found love again and put it into action.*

*With an unshakable belief in kindness,
hope for a brighter future and a loving
desire to make a difference, Kiss A Me
teaches us all...that everyone can.*

KISS A ME was happy
Enjoying the day.
He was watching birds fly
And the dolphins at play.

He was suddenly startled
By a cry from below.
The birds quickly settled,
And the dolphins swam slow.

KISS A ME dove swiftly
And searched far and near,
For the cry that he heard
Came from someone in fear.

As he quickly descended,
A wreck came in view.
There, close beside it,
Were seals, quite a few.

When KISS A ME drew close,
The seals backed up in awe.
There one little seal lay
Crying on the ocean floor.

"I swam through some water
That was turbid, not clear.
It got in my nose,
In my throat, in my ear.

"And now I can tell you
I'm not feeling well.
I'm feeling quite sick.
I can't swim, taste, or smell.

"I can't rise for the air
That I desperately need.
While I live in the water,
I'm a mammal, I breathe."

"Seal, rest for a moment,
Your end's not yet here.
I'm strong, I can lift you.
You're safe - have no fear."

KISS A ME thought quickly
As he looked all around.
He spied a ship's rope
From the wreck on the ground.

He tore the rope free
From where it was tied
And worked quickly to secure
The little seal to his side.

KISS A ME rose gently
With the sick little seal
And swam with him slowly
Toward the safe place to heal.

"Now back at the surface,
For the air you must breathe,
We'll tend to your illness
With the good care you need.

"There is a place of protection
Where sick creatures can go.
The people there will help you.
I'll pull you in tow.

"In this place of protection
People are loving and true.
They care for sea creatures
And mammals like you.

"There are large tanks of water
That are kept clear and blue.
In one of the tanks
They will gently place you.

"You'll be close to the surface,
So the air that you need
Will always be near you,
And on fresh fish you'll feed."

"Thank you, little whale,
For being loving and true.
I will remember forever
How much I owe you.

"I don't know what happened
To make me so ill.
Though I tried hard to rise,
I just lay sick and still."

"The water you swam in,
That you saw wasn't clear,
Infected your nose,
Your throat, and your ear.

"In recovery they will treat you
'Til you're well on your way
To good health and happiness
And can frolic and play.

"When you swim free,
Remember and tell
The other sick creatures
Where you were made well.

"The people at recovery
Who work night and day
Will teach all the people
What creatures can't say.

"For we all need the water
Made pure, clean, and free,
And that will be done
When people control their debris.

"And we will reward them
For all good that they do.
We will feed and refresh them
And swim with them too."

Now...

If someday, when you're older,
A troubled creature comes to view,
Remember your friend KISS A ME
And the caring he taught you.

KISS A ME loves you...Pass it on!

THE END

Babette Douglas, a talented poet and artist, has
written over 30 children's books in which diverse
creatures live together in harmony, friendship
and respect. She brings to her delightful stories
the insights and caring accumulated in a lifetime
of varied experiences.

"I believe strongly in the healing power of love,"
she says. "I want to empower children to see
with their hearts and to love all the creatures of
the earth, including themselves." The unique
stories told by her "teacher creatures" enable
children to learn to recognize their own gifts and
to value tolerance, compassion, optimism and
perseverance.

Ms. Douglas, who was born and educated in
New York City, has lived in Sayville, New York
for over forty years.

Additional Kiss A Me™ teacher-creature stories:

AMAZING GRACE

BLUE WISE

CURLY HARE

FALCON EDDIE

THE FLUTTERBY

KISS A ME: *A Little Whale Watching*

KISS A ME *Goes to School*

LARKSPUR

THE LYON BEAR™

THE LYON BEAR™ *deTails*

THE LYON BEAR™: *The Mane Event*

MISS EVONNE *And the Mice of Nice*

MISS TEAK *And the Endorphins*

NOREEN: *The Real King of the Jungle*

OSCARPUS

ROSEBUD

SQUIRT: *The Magic Cuddle Fish*

**Character toys are available for each book.
For additional information on books, toys,
and other products visit us at:**

www.kissame.com